HIDDEN
IN PLAIN
SIGHT

For Ben and Jack, my two "wise" guys—
and Shelby, the girl they love.

HIDDEN IN PLAIN SIGHT

MYSTERIES OF ECKERT HOUSE

by CHRIS AUER

smarter • stronger
2:52
deeper • cooler

Zonderkidz

Zonder**kidz**.

The children's group of Zondervan

www.zonderkidz.com

Hidden in Plain Sight
Copyright © 2004 by Chris Auer

Requests for information should be addressed to:
Zonderkidz, Grand Rapids, Michigan 49530

Library of Congress Cataloging-in-Publication Data

Auer, Chris, 1955-
  Hidden in plain sight / by Chris Auer.
    p. cm.–(2:52 mysteries of Eckert House ; bk. 1)
  Summary: Twelve-year-old Dan tries to apply a scripture passage to the events of his
life when, while working at an antebellum mansion that serves as a museum, he digs
up a skeleton and convinces his cousin and a friend to help him learn who was buried
and by whom.
  ISBN 0-310-70870-2 (softcover)
  [1. Skeleton—Fiction. 2. Museums—Fiction. 3. Christian life—Fiction. 4. Mystery
and detective stories.] I. Title.
  PZ7.A9113Hi 2005
  [Fic]–dc22
                            2003027958

Editor: Amy DeVries
Cover design: Jay Smith–Juicebox Designs
Interior design: Susan Ambs
Art direction: Michelle Lenger and Merit Alderink

Printed in the United States of America

05 06 07 /❖DCI/ 10 9 8 7 6 5 4 3 2 1

CONTENTS

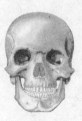

THE COLLISION

Whenever Dan Pruitt was unhappy, he'd jump on his skateboard and head over to the west side of town where the hills were steeper and the sidewalks were smoother. Lately, Dan had spent a lot of time on his skateboard.

Unhappiness was something new to Dan. Although he was a kid who seldom felt sorry for himself, he had more than a few good reasons to be upset. As he picked up speed on the half-mile-long slope down Filkins Street, he thought about all that had happened since spring. Three months ago, his father, who flew F–18 Tomcats for the Navy, had been sent overseas. Taking off and landing on an aircraft carrier was dangerous enough, but now he was flying missions where the enemy was shooting at him.

"Don't worry, Dan," his father had said as he hugged him good-bye, "I'm in God's hands."

Dan tried not to worry, but he couldn't help thinking that even people who trust in God get hurt. Or worse.

Then, almost as soon as his dad shipped out, Dan's mother announced they were moving to Freemont, Pennsylvania, the town near Pittsburgh where she had grown up. Dan had tried to tell his mother how he'd miss his friends and his school, and how his baseball team needed him, but it didn't make any difference.

"Grandpa Mike needs our help," she had replied.

Dan really couldn't argue with that. His grandfather had always been one of Dan's favorite people, always ready for an adventure, always telling jokes.

"Hey, Dan, I've got a good one for you," Grandpa Mike would say every time he saw him. Then he would throw out one joke after another.

"How do you know if you have a tough mosquito? You slap him and he slaps you back!

"What was the snail doing on the highway? About one mile a day.

"What's green and brown and can kill you if it falls out of a tree? A pool table!"

But now Grandpa Mike had difficulty saying anything and rarely came out of his room. He had had a stroke. And Dan didn't know how to help his grandfather.

Dan's skateboard started to pick up speed when he got to the new section of sidewalk on Filkins Street. That was good, because the faster he went, the less he had to think.

"Hey, Dan! Dan! Wait up!" his cousin Pete called from across the street.

"Can't!" Dan called over his shoulder. "Meet me at the park!"

Dan knew he'd taken a chance going by Pete's house. He didn't want Pete to see him. Both Pete and Dan were twelve. In the past, when Dan visited Pete, they'd gotten along great. Really great. They loved visiting each other. But visiting Pete was different from living in the same town with him. Pete was small for his age, and, as Dan soon discovered, he was one of those kids that other guys liked to pick on.

"Why do you let them call you names and push you around like that?" Dan had demanded after a shoving match with a couple of older boys on the basketball court.

"It's no big deal," Pete had insisted.

But it was to Dan. It was a big deal because Dan tried to stop it and Pete wouldn't let him. It was a big deal because it embarrassed Dan to see that his own cousin was so weak. And because deep down Dan knew it really *did* bother Pete.

"Chances are he won't show up at the park," Dan mumbled to himself as he reached the halfway point of the hill. He had also reached top speed. The wind in his face felt great.

The people who lived in Freemont often said their town looked like something you'd see on a picture postcard. It was true. Big trees arched over the streets. There were a lot of picket fences—all gleaming white, of course—and the lawns they protected looked more like green carpet than grass. The houses were as well kept as the yards. The overall effect of Freemont was a place of peace and quiet and order.

Dan Pruitt on a skateboard, however, was the opposite of peace and quiet and order. He swooped in and out of parked cars. He dodged pedestrians.

He managed to get his skateboard up on railings and under benches. One afternoon he even played tennis on his skateboard, beating six kids and three very amused adults.

Dan was approaching the bottom of the hill where Filkins Street ends abruptly at Golden Street. On his right was the biggest house in Freemont, a Victorian mansion called Eckert House. Eckert House had once been the home of the richest family in town, but now it was a museum. Dan liked to race past it not only because of the challenge of the hill but because he liked to imagine that the Eckerts still lived there, and that one of them, a pretty girl about his age, watched for him. One day, he imagined, she would be waiting for him outside the large iron gate as he careened around the corner, and she would jump into his arms and . . .

"You are such a loser," Dan said aloud to himself. He crouched a little lower to get ready for the corner. Making the turn was a matter of hooking his arm around the sign pole and then leaning out as far as he could as he guided his skateboard ninety degrees to the right. Whoosh! He made the turn with ease. He released his arm, straightened up, and, still clipping along at a good pace, headed down Golden Street.

Suddenly a figure stepped through the iron gate of Eckert House and out onto the sidewalk directly in front of Dan. Dan tried to veer to the left, but he was too close. A split second before the collision, Dan realized with horror that he was about to hit Miss Alma Louise Stockton LeMay.

Although she stood only five feet tall and couldn't have weighed more than ninety pounds, and although she was older than seventy (no one knew exactly how old), Miss Alma Louise Stockton LeMay struck terror in the hearts of everyone in Freemont. She was the curator of Eckert House, where she ruled over its displays and artifacts like a grand queen. Miss Alma never smiled and never ever answered a question with four or five words when one would do.

Somehow Dan's arm got caught in the strap of the large purse that hung from her shoulder, and somehow, either because of his speed or the angle at which they collided, she ended up on his back.

Miss Alma started screaming.

"Put me down this instant! Help! Police!"

Even then, Dan might have gotten Miss Alma safely to the ground, but for some reason, she decided that the best place for her hands was over his eyes.

"No!" he yelled, meaning that he could no longer see.

"Yes!" she yelled back, thinking he was refusing to stop.

Those who saw the whole thing from the park across the street were impressed by two things: one, that the boy on the skateboard managed to stay upright with an elderly woman wrapped around his shoulders and head, and two, that the elderly woman seemed more angry than scared. Miss Alma was so busy pounding his helmet with her fist that she didn't realize they were in the street and that two cars had swerved to miss them. Dan was doing very well considering that he could catch only brief glimpses of the street ahead as his helmet bounced up and down in front of his eyes. He made it across the street and into the little park that ran along the bank of Morgan River. He hoped to find a nice soft patch of grass where he could set Miss Alma down, but she made this impossible by pushing his helmet even farther down on his head until it finally covered his eyes. When Dan felt the sidewalk in the park slope down and they started to pick up speed, he knew they were headed for even more trouble.

"Let go of me!" she demanded. Her knees were now on his shoulders and she was waving her arms over her head. They looked like a couple of crazed cheerleaders.

"No!" Dan shouted back, and this time he really meant "no," for if he let go of her, she might get seriously hurt. A moment later the wheels of his skateboard stopped making the smooth noise they always make on concrete, and instead started rumbling over planks of wood. That could mean only one thing: They were on the little dock that juts out into the river. Five seconds later the wheels of the skateboard weren't making any noise at all. Dan and Miss Alma were airborne. They hit the water with a loud splash, Miss Alma letting out a long, shrill scream from the time they left the dock until they hit the water.

One surprised little girl playing with her brother in the park thought it was some kind of performance and started to clap. Others joined in, and applause was the first sound that greeted Miss Alma when she came up for air. She glared at the onlookers. They stopped clapping. For a split second, Dan considered *not* coming up for air, but good sense got the better of him and he made his way to the surface.

"Young man," Miss Alma sputtered, "I don't know who you are or what you think you were doing, but when you get out of jail, do me a favor and don't bother explaining it to me."

Jail! Well, why not, thought Dan. Could it be any worse than what he was already going through?

"Take me away," he answered. "The sooner the better."

THE
DISCOVERY

The next day, Dan stood trembling in the entrance hall of Eckert House. He was waiting for Miss Alma to make her appearance and pass judgment on him. His own mother had handed him over to her without so much as an ounce of mercy.

"You're way too reckless on that skateboard, and we're lucky she didn't call the police," had been his mother's cool comment. She had then informed Dan that he was to *walk* (she especially stressed that part) over to Eckert House and accept whatever punishment Miss Alma thought was fair. As Dan waited, he was sure "fair" to Miss Alma would involve pain, humiliation, more pain, and then more humiliation.

The inside of the museum was just as impressive as the outside. The large front hall was covered with shiny parquet flooring. The floor was so shiny, in fact, that Dan could look down and see his reflection. He leaned over and made a face at himself.

"Miss Alma has to finish an important phone call and then she'll be right down," said an elderly woman all dressed in gray. Her name was Mrs. Doheny, and her job was to sit behind a small desk at the side of the hall and greet everyone who came through the front door.

"Great," said Dan, not meaning it at all, and offering her a smile that only showed how nervous he was. Mrs. Doheny smiled back in the same way. It made Dan think that she, too, was afraid of Miss Alma.

Opening off the hall to the left was the biggest room in the house. It had once been the Main Salon, which Dan knew was just a fancy name for the living room. To the right were the library and the Little Salon, which was another fancy name for the family room. Down the hall was a dining room. All of the rooms held exhibits of one kind or another, as did some of the rooms on the second floor. The third floor was off-limits to the public.

A portrait of Julius Eckert, the original owner of Eckert House, hung over the staircase. He had made millions building railroads. He had built this mansion just after the Civil War and then traveled around the world three times buying things to fill it. He brought back anything he found interesting: suits of armor, paintings, sculpture, shrunken heads, Chinese screens, stuffed animals, clocks, mummies, rare books, enormous insects pinned to cardboard — anything and everything.

While Julius was good at spending money, he was, apparently, the only Eckert who ever considered *making* money. Even millions of dollars, managed unwisely, will last only so long. As it turned out, the money lasted a little over a hundred years. That's when Marie, the very last Eckert to live in Eckert House, couldn't pay her bills anymore. So she gave Eckert House and everything in it to the town, then climbed into her rickety old Volkswagen "Bug" and drove away. She was never heard from again.

Two years later, Eckert House opened its doors as a museum. Everything on display in Eckert House had once belonged to the family. The museum was never going to be as famous as the Smithsonian, but a lot of people came from all over the country to see it, and it became famous in its own quiet kind of way.

What wasn't quiet was Miss Alma's shrill, angry voice. It could be heard all the way from the third floor. Her "private" phone conversation was no longer private.

"You cannot borrow that painting. I don't care if it is for your office in Washington, Senator. Eckert House is a private museum, not a lending library."

Mrs. Doheny looked at Dan and there was no mistaking the look of pure terror in her eyes.

"I think I'll wait in there," Dan said as he pointed to the library. In the back of his mind he was hoping that maybe, just maybe, if he hid in an out-of-the-way corner, Miss Alma would forget all about their appointment.

Dan chose a spot near a display case that featured invitations and photographs from some of the elaborate parties the Eckerts had thrown in the late 1800s and early 1900s.

Eckert House was famous for its fancy balls and parties. Royalty from Europe had visited, and once, in 1897, even the vice president of the United States had been a guest. There was one picture where everyone was dressed in white, another where everyone was dressed in black, and one where everyone, even the women, were dressed as Sherlock Holmes. The framed invitation next to that photo promised a "whopping mystery" as well as "a whopping good timc" and a "whopping feast."

Apparently the word "whopping" was very popular in 1901, Dan thought.

"Right now I'd settle for a whopping escape," he muttered.

"I'll bet you would," cracked the voice that only a few minutes before had been scolding one of the most important people in Washington, D.C. Miss Alma's steely blue eyes peered at Dan over the tops of her glasses. Dan straightened up as if he were a sailor in the presence of an admiral. Something about her manner almost made him salute.

"Daniel Pruitt, ma'am," he said.

"I'm aware of who you are. And while I'm thrilled to see that there are no wheels anywhere near your feet, in my day, a gentleman removed his hat when he entered a building."

Dan snatched the baseball cap off his head and,

before he realized what he was doing, he spit into the palm of his hand and slicked down his hair.

"How charming," Miss Alma said, clearly not charmed in the least. She turned and walked away, motioning for Dan to follow her. As he passed a stuffed moose head that was mounted on the wall, he imagined his own head taking its place if he did not do everything he was told.

Miss Alma gave Dan a list of chores she estimated would take him a hundred hours to complete. Normally the chores would have been done by Rick Doheny, the caretaker of Eckert House and the son of the frightened little woman who sat behind the desk in the hall, but he was sick.

"I think the punishment fits the crime, don't you?" she declared, daring him to challenge her.

Dan estimated that to do everything on her list would take him more like a hundred days, not a hundred hours, but he kept his mouth shut. He remembered something his father had said to him just before he left: "I'm going to give you a Scripture to think about while I'm gone, Danny. It's Luke, chapter 2, verse 52, 'And Jesus grew in wisdom and stature, and in favor with God and men.' It's never too early to start thinking and acting like a man instead of a boy."

Dan seriously doubted that Jesus had anyone in his life as difficult as Miss Alma when he was twelve, but he made a solemn promise to be polite to her no matter what she said or did. And, in the next few days, did she ever have a lot to say.

"When you trim the hedges, I don't want to see so much as a *leaf* on the sidewalk," Miss Alma complained as she picked up a few stray twigs Dan had left behind.

"The grass on the lawn is to be cut to a height of *exactly* one and a half inches," she informed him as she measured the grass with a ruler.

"All weeds are to be pulled out by their *roots*." Unhappy with Dan's efforts, she demonstrated the proper technique.

Dan listened carefully and did his best to follow what seemed like hundreds and hundreds of instructions. But one afternoon he couldn't take it anymore. He snapped. There was an overgrown area behind the formal garden that Miss Alma wanted him to clear of brush and rotting leaves. In the middle of the tangle was a small fountain topped with a bronze statue of what may have been an angel or a young girl . . . or maybe even a Greek god.

The fountain had been unused for years, and weeds and vines choked everything, including the bronze statue. Miss Alma was convinced that once the brush was cut back, the weeds were cleared away, and the fountain was repaired, the area would be a delightful place for visitors to sit and have tea. Dan could not have cared less about whether visitors sipped tea or went home thirsty. He was willing to clear away the brush, but he drew the line at what Miss Alma called a weed but what he was sure was a small tree. It was growing right next to the fountain.

"It's a tree," Dan insisted, mostly because he didn't want to dig the thing up. "It's a tree and it should be allowed to grow where God intended it to grow."

"It's a weed," Miss Alma shot back. "And even if it *is* a tree, if I say it's a weed, then to you it's a weed."

Dan lost the argument. A few minutes later he was muttering to himself and swinging a pickax to get at the roots. He imagined tossing the ugly little statue into the garbage, covering Miss Alma with concrete, and placing her on top of the fountain instead.

The ax struck a rock, and Dan reached down with both hands and pulled it out of the way. He struck another and another and another, tossing them all onto the pile of rubble that he would have to cart away when he was through.

Dan wasn't the best science student ever born, and geology — with the exception of volcanoes — was to him, in a word, boring. But the rocks he was hitting and tossing away were interesting. They were unlike any he had ever seen before — smooth and white with odd shapes. Not like rocks at all. He stopped to study the next one he dug up.

Something was wrong. Whatever he was holding was definitely not a rock. He looked at the pieces he had tossed away. He looked down into the hole he was digging. He got down on his knees and pushed away the dirt with his bare hands. His hands touched something smooth and curved, and there, staring up at him from the moist earth, was a human skull. Dan had been digging up a skeleton.

THE
THREAT

The police came to Eckert House, sirens announcing their arrival. Miss Alma was as unafraid of them as she was of the senator.

"I'm watching you, and if anything is out of place, I'll see that you're locked up in your own jail," she warned. She then turned to Dan. "What did you do?" She demanded.

"Me?!" he exclaimed.

But Miss Alma wasn't interested in his answer. News of the discovery of the skeleton had spread quickly. Even Miss Alma wasn't able to prevent a television reporter from interviewing—as they put it on TV—"Young Daniel Pruitt, whose gruesome discovery has shaken this sleepy town to its very core."

Dan's mother let him stay up that night to watch himself on the eleven o'clock news. He thought the whole thing was pretty cool.

The next morning, Dan and his cousin Pete sat on Pete's front steps looking down the hill toward Eckert House. There was still a small crowd gathered at the corner. They couldn't get any closer because the police had sealed off the area as a crime scene, and Miss Alma had closed the museum.

A girl their age left the group and started walking up the street toward them. She was small and wiry, with a no-nonsense haircut and an attitude to match. It was their friend Shelby Foster. Dan never called her Shelby, though. To him, she was "Search Engine," much to her annoyance. Dan called her that because there wasn't anything she couldn't find out if she put her mind to it.

Shelby, more than anyone else, was the person who kept Dan and Pete together. She liked them both. A lot. She knew how frustrated Dan got when Pete let himself get pushed around. She had noticed that Pete was learning to stand up for himself a little and believed Dan had a lot to do with the change. She thought Pete was a good influence on his more rambunctious cousin.

Pete was one of those guys who took the "whole God thing"—as Shelby put it—seriously. Shelby didn't buy into it much herself—God seemed too far away—but she couldn't deny that it had helped Pete cope when his mother ran off a few years back and even now when his father couldn't hold down a steady job. She saw that Pete's kind of faith was good for Dan, too. Dan was always calmer when Pete talked about how much he trusted God.

"Nice picture," Shelby said as she dropped the newspaper she was carrying at Dan's feet. His picture was on the front page. The photographer had snapped Dan standing near the exposed skeleton and had artfully made the creepy weed- and vine-covered statue on the fountain seem to loom over him. The headline read: "Death Stalks Local Boy." Dan had already seen the morning paper. In fact he had gone out and bought ten copies.

"Shall I autograph it?" Dan asked.

"If you want to," she answered. "It might impress my cat when I use it to line his litter box."

"You can autograph mine," Pete offered. Unlike Shelby, Pete was serious.

A car coming up the hill honked its horn. Dan automatically stood up and waved, realizing a moment later that the horn had been for Chester, Pete's enormous cat, who liked to lie in the middle of the street and force cars to drive around him.

"Look who's playing the celebrity," groaned Shelby. She suggested they go around back so Dan's "public" wouldn't disturb them.

They often climbed a big tree in Pete's backyard when they had important matters to discuss. Now, as soon as they were up in its branches, Dan told Shelby and Pete all about discovering the skeleton. He couldn't resist adding a few creative touches, such as the sickening sound of the pickax when it hit the first bone. But all in all, what he told his friends was pretty much what he had told the police and then the reporters.

He did have one extra bit of information, however. Something he had overheard one of the policemen say to Miss Alma. "He looked at the skeleton, then looked up at the house, then right at Miss Alma and said, 'Maybe this will answer the questions some of us have had over the years.'

"Miss Alma looked right back at him and said, 'Let the dead rest in peace.' Those were her exact words. 'Let the dead rest in peace.' It gave me the creeps."

Shelby and Pete exchanged a look. Dan saw that they knew something he didn't.

"What?"

What Dan heard in the next few minutes changed Dan's life, and, as a result, Shelby's and Pete's as well.

Over the years a lot of strange stories were told about Eckert House and the people who lived there. Some stories were stranger and harder to believe than others.

One story, as Dan now heard, was the rumor that one of the Eckerts, David Eckert, had been kept locked in a special room in the attic. Townsfolk said he was a danger to himself and to others. Then in 1943 he disappeared. No one ever saw him again. About the same time another young man in the town disappeared. The story that got around was that David Eckert had murdered the young man, and then he was murdered by someone in the young man's family. But no one ever knew for sure.

What the people of Freemont believed was that the Eckerts had somehow managed to hide the truth— maybe by paying off the other family. "The Eckerts wanted to cover up what had happened," Shelby said, "so they convinced the victim's family to stay quiet and they never told the police or anyone else about David's death. They just didn't talk about it."

Dan was amazed. This was all new to him.

"Remember when you were visiting a couple of summers ago," Pete said, "and some kids snuck over the fence at Eckert House and dug a big hole right next to the spruce tree?"

Dan remembered. He also remembered that at the time he was more interested in fishing on the river than in some nutty kids digging a hole.

"That tree was planted in the early '40s, and rumor has it that the Eckerts put it over David's body. Those kids were looking for David Eckert."

"Why didn't you guys tell me before?"

"They were just stupid stories," Shelby said. Shelby's impatience with anything but the facts was well known to Dan.

"Gossip," Pete added. "But now that there *is* a body on the property, and you found it, well, that changes everything."

Dan got a look in his eyes that Pete and Shelby knew they had to wait out. In silence. He was formulating a plan.

"Okay, this is the deal," Dan said. "This has been the worst summer ever. I need to do something. If I have to jump one more time when Miss Alma says jump, I'll go crazy. You, Search Engine, need to get that brain of yours away from the computer and out into the real world. And Pete, old boy, old cousin, old friend, you need to be the toughest kid in school when school starts in a few weeks."

Pete blushed.

"I happen to think my computer is more interesting than most of the people I know," Shelby said, looking right at Dan.

"Fine. But when Pete and I make the cover of all the magazines and are interviewed on every network, don't forget you could have been right there with us." Dan scooted over next to his cousin and put his arm around Pete's shoulders to emphasize his point.

Pete swallowed hard. "We're gonna do all that?"

"Yup."

"How?"

"We're gonna solve the mystery of who David Eckert killed and who killed him. And we're gonna do it before the police do."

For the next hour, Dan explained his plan. Even Shelby had to admit Dan was making sense. Miss

Alma, to make things easier for Dan, had given him the caretaker's keys. The keys opened most of the doors in Eckert House. Dan was convinced that somewhere in the files and boxes and treasures the public never saw was information about David that would lead them to his killer. With the keys, they could do a thorough search.

"Plus, we're kids," Dan added. "Who's gonna think we're up to anything?"

Dan got an answer to his question that afternoon. An envelope with his name written on it was in the mailbox. He took it out, ripped open the envelope, and saw a note and a photograph. The picture was of Dan, Pete, and Shelby, and it had been taken that morning, just a few hours ago, from across the street from Pete's house, when they had all been sitting on Pete's front porch.

Dan studied the envelope carefully. There was no return address, and although there was a stamp in the upper right-hand corner, it had not been canceled at the post office. That meant the sender had put it in the mailbox. Dan unfolded the note. "Thanks for the help. Now stay out of my way—especially if you don't want to get hurt. As you can see, I know a lot about you."

Something inside Dan told him that the threat was not a joke. Somehow he knew that the person who had written the note was serious.

He was right.

THE TOWER

The next morning Dan went into his grandfather's room to read to him from the Bible and the sports page of the newspaper. He did this every morning. Before the stroke, Grandpa Mike would listen to Dan read and then always make a connection between whatever was happening with the Pittsburgh Pirates and the passage of Scripture he was studying.

Dan read out loud from Philippians, "Do nothing out of selfish ambition or vain conceit, but in humility consider others better than yourselves." He smiled. Grandpa Mike would have said that's just what a ballplayer needs to do, too: Play for the team, not for himself.

Dan put the Bible on his lap. "I understand all that, Grandpa, but aren't there times when a guy needs to claim something for himself? I mean, I miss my old friends. I miss my dad. I even miss my room at the old house. Is it wrong to want something that is just mine?"

Grandpa Mike looked at Dan. He couldn't speak, but Dan thought he could see in his grandfather's eyes that he understood.

Of course, Grandpa Mike could have no way of knowing that Dan was talking about investigating the mystery of David Eckert and that he had convinced himself it was okay to keep the whole investigation a secret. Having a secret made Dan feel special—and right then he needed to feel special.

"Besides," he added, "if I'm going to 'grow in wisdom' like Luke 2:52 says, I have to learn how to handle things on my own, right?" Dan kissed Grandpa Mike on the forehead and left, feeling very much in charge of his own life.

Miss Alma was not in charge of Eckert House anymore, at least not until the police finished their investigation. The grass went uncut and the bushes remained untrimmed, and Dan couldn't have been happier.

"Since it's impossible for me to do any work outside, maybe there's something I can do for you inside," he offered.

Miss Alma studied him for a moment. Dan *knew* it was impossible for one person to read another's mind, but then again, this was Miss Alma, and if anyone gave the impression that it could be done, it was Miss Alma. As he stood there, he tried to not even think about his plans to secretly explore Eckert House.

Twenty minutes later, Dan was in the little basement beneath the big basement staring at a pile of wooden crates.

"You can move these to the third floor," Miss Alma told him. She stressed that he was to use the back stairs and he was not, under any circumstances, to make noise.

"I think we both agree you've done enough to turn things upside down here." After making that observation, she walked away.

Carrying all those boxes to the third floor was hard work, but Dan didn't mind. He had his very own set of keys, and every time he dropped a box off, he looked over his shoulder and, if no one was around, he'd try opening another door. Most of the rooms were old bedrooms where shelves had been built to hold all of Julius Eckert's treasures. They were interesting and, under normal circumstances, Dan would have loved to take more time with one of the antique Swiss clocks, or the ancient sword, or even the Chinese puppets. But he was a man on a mission, and his mission was to find something to crack open the mystery of David Eckert.

On his seventh trip to the third floor, he found it. He unlocked a door at the end of the hall and discovered a staircase. After looking back down the hall to make sure that no one was around, he stepped in and closed the door behind him.

The air was stuffy. It was hard to breathe. Dan's heart was beating very fast. He took a few deep breaths to calm himself before starting up the twisting stairs.

Daylight was coming in from the attic above, but it was dark on the stairway and Dan had to feel his way along the wall. About halfway up, his hand touched a doorknob.

"Why would there be a door in the middle of a staircase?" he wondered aloud. He turned the knob.

It was locked. As he looked down to get his keys, he saw a tiny sliver of light on his hand and realized the light was coming through a keyhole. He got down on one knee to look through the tiny opening into the room on the other side of the door.

The room Dan saw through the keyhole was round. He realized it was part of the small tower on the north side of the house, a tower that was hard to see from the street because a large chimney blocked it from view. There was no furniture. The room was empty. Dan tried the doorknob again and pushed. The door was definitely locked.

Dan stood there, thinking. Then he remembered one particular key on the caretaker's key ring. The key didn't look like any of the others, and he had not used it to test any of the doors on the third floor because it simply would not have fit.

"I wonder . . . ," he whispered.

He got down on his knees in front of the keyhole and used the light peeking through to find the strange key. His hands were shaking and he dropped the key ring. He picked it up and dropped it again.

"Smooth," he grumbled as he finally found the key. He took a deep breath and slipped the key into the lock. It fit! He turned the key. There was a loud click—the sound of a sliding bolt. Dan tried the doorknob again. This time it turned freely in his hand and the door flew open as if on a spring.

He stepped into the room, blinking as his eyes adjusted to the sunlight streaming through the windows. He sneezed.

Dan moved to the center of the room and turned completely around. The room was empty. But he wondered if he could find a clue that would tell him what this room had been used for. He was sure it was connected to David Eckert because he remembered what Miss Alma had done when she was talking with the policeman. When she told the policeman to "let the dead rest in peace," she had looked up at the tower.

Dan walked to the windows to look down at the spot where the skeleton had been discovered. Something on the wall caught his eye—a brownish smudge. As he bent to examine it, he was positive it was dried blood. It appeared to be very, very old. And there was something else nearby too—something scratched into the wooden floor. He blew away the dust and read a name: "Davey."

He was real! He was here! his mind screamed at him.

Down below, Miss Alma called his name. Dan jumped to his feet. He knew he couldn't be caught in this room or even on the staircase. He hurried to the door and shut and locked it behind him. He was once again on the stairs.

"Mr. Pruitt!" called Miss Alma from just outside the door at the bottom of the attic stairs. Dan was fairly sure he'd locked the door behind him. He thought if he didn't move, she would look elsewhere for him. Then a loud creak and a bright shaft of light told him that she had opened the door.

"Mr. Pruitt!"

The curve of the staircase kept her from seeing him, but Dan flattened himself against the wall just the same.

If she really thought I was up here, Dan thought, *she'd already be climbing the stairs.*

The sound was unmistakable. Miss Alma was climbing the stairs. Dan had two choices: make a mad dash to the attic and hope to find a hiding place or go back down the stairs into the full force of Miss Alma's anger. He wished he had time to unlock the door to the secret room and hide in there, but he didn't.

"Mr. Pruitt!" she called again with more than a hint of anger in her voice. She took another two steps. In desperation, he pushed himself hard against the wall in the deepest shadow he could find. *Maybe she won't see me,* he thought.

He wasn't sure how it happened, or even what happened, but the next thing he knew, the wall behind him moved—slid really—and he found that he was no longer on the staircase to the attic. Instead he was on a different staircase, a secret staircase that ran alongside the other one, except inside the wall.

Dan was more surprised than scared. He stayed very still as he heard Miss Alma pass him on the other side of the wall. She went up into the attic, called his name again, then went back down to the third floor, the second, and finally to the first floor.

When he was absolutely sure she was gone, he pushed against the wall where it had slid open. He expected the wall to open so he could get back out onto the other staircase. But the wall did not budge. He pushed again, harder this time. Again, the wall would not move.

He stood there in the darkness. No one knew where he was. He needed to find a way out.

"The next time you do something like this, bring a flashlight, Genius," he muttered to himself. Gradually his eyes adjusted to the darkness and Dan noticed a weak, grayish light seeping in from somewhere above him. He started down the stairs.

The secret staircase wound round and round a brick wall. Every ten or twelve steps the stairs had what seemed like a landing. At each one, Dan pushed against the outside wall, hoping to find another sliding door. As he made his way down, he realized that the stairs had been built around the big chimney for the fireplace in the Main Salon. Dan figured he was near the first floor when the chimney got wider and he heard voices on the other side. He heard his name. They were talking about him.

"When you see him, tell him to wait for me in the front hall."

"Yes, Miss Alma."

"And don't talk to him yourself."

"No, Miss Alma."

"And I want to move this suit of armor down to room 8B in the basement. It's the silliest thing we have in this museum. Imagine a grown man wearing a tin can, riding a horse, and waving a sword. I hope that expert from Germany who's coming next week will buy it and get it out of here."

"Yes, Miss Alma."

The talk about the suit of armor convinced Dan he was down to the first floor. That's where the armor was on display—in the Main Salon. The armor was Dan's favorite display in Eckert House. He often imagined himself putting it on, jumping on his skateboard, and whizzing through town, waving at everybody.

Dan figured that if the secret staircase had an exit anywhere, it would be in the Main Salon. When he got to the bottom, he felt along the wall very carefully, trying to find a lever or a doorknob or something that would get him out. When he found a hinge, he knew he was close. A few feet to the left he found three holes, something like the holes in a bowling ball. He put his thumb and two fingers in the holes, just as if he were bowling, and squeezed. He heard a loud click and a panel swung open. He stepped out into the Main Salon.

The fireplace itself jutted out into the room a good four feet, and the secret door opened at the back of its far corner. The door was placed in such a way that it was possible to slip in or out without being seen. Dan closed the door behind him and moved as quietly as he could to the front hall.

Mrs. Doheny was not at her desk. Dan slipped into an ancient armchair just outside the Main Salon and told himself to look bored. Bored? With a secret room, dried blood, a name scratched on the floor, *and* a secret passageway? *Yes,* he repeated silently, *bored.* He did not want Miss Alma to start asking any questions.

Dan practiced yawning. A practice yawn turned into a real one just as Miss Alma came out of the library.

"Hand over your mouth, Mr. Pruitt," she snapped. "I have no desire to see your tonsils."

Dan jumped to his feet.

"You wanted to talk to me?" Again, he almost felt that he should salute her.

Miss Alma studied him for a moment.

"I'm going down to the police station. More of this distasteful business. When you're done with those crates, you may go out and bring in all the tools you were using when — when you started all of this. The police said they are finally done out there."

Miss Alma was almost out the front door when Dan called to her. He was tired of being blamed for what had happened.

"Miss Alma, I didn't start anything. I was only doing what you told me to do."

Miss Alma stopped.

"Yes, you were," she stated.

Dan felt relief. He hoped that would be the end of it.

"You know what I find interesting, Mr. Pruitt?" she continued, clearly not expecting an answer from him. "I find it interesting that I told Mrs. Doheny that I wanted to see you, and then we both went into the library. She's still in there. I know for a fact that she hasn't talked to you."

With that, Miss Alma turned and left.

Dan didn't move for a full two minutes. Did she know where he had been and what he had been doing? Did she know he had overheard her conversation from inside the wall? And if she did know, why hadn't she just said so? Dan realized that he would have to be very careful from now on. He also wondered if Miss Alma had a few secrets of her own, things she didn't want anyone else to know.

THE SWITCH

Dan finished picking up the tools he had been using when he dug up the skeleton. He was convinced that Miss Alma knew exactly who had been buried in that hole—and why. Dan himself was sure that it was David Eckert.

The stone gardening shed where the tools were stored was built right into the high wall that marked the northern edge of the Eckert property. As Dan closed and locked the shed door, he heard someone call his name.

"Pssst! Pruitt! Hey, Dan!"

Dan looked around. He finally saw Jesse Crane lying on top of the ten-foot-high wall.

"How did you get up th—" Dan stopped when he saw Jesse reach over the other side of the wall and help someone up. Jesse's twin brother, Dylan, poked his head up and climbed up on the wall. Dylan had obviously boosted Jesse up first and then Jesse gave Dylan a hand.

Jesse and Dylan were the two guys in Freemont whom Dan wanted most as friends. They were the most popular kids his age in town, and Dan wanted to belong to their crowd. He wanted it a lot. Which was why, instead of telling the twins they couldn't come onto the property, he helped them down off the wall and offered to show them where he had found the skeleton.

"Wow!" said Dylan as he looked into the empty hole. "Was there any blood?"

"What did it smell like?" Jesse wanted to know. "Did it make you sick?"

Dan's version of the story this time was quite different. Since he now had heard the legend of the murder, he told Jesse and Dylan that he had thought the fountain was the most logical place to look for the body.

Jesse and Dylan were impressed. However, since now there was only a hole *without* a body, there wasn't much to look at. Jesse, being the kind of kid who always wants something to be happening, started fooling around. He jumped up on the fountain and put his arm around the statue.

"Look! Local boy stalks death!" he yelled, making fun of the headline that had been in the newspaper just a few days before. "Take *that!*" he said as he gave the statue a shove. Dan let out a yell. The statue rocked back and forth and then toppled over with a thud.

"Gotta go!" Dylan called over his shoulder as he and Jesse ran to the wall and scampered up and over as fast as possible.

"Hey! Come back! I need a little help here!" Dan's calls were useless. The twins were gone.

When Dan stepped up into the fountain to set the statue upright again, he saw a dent on its outstretched arm.

"Great, not only are you ugly, but now you're broken," he muttered to the statue as if it could hear him.

Dan didn't know what to do. Should he tell Miss Alma that a statue that was essentially worthless was broken? Probably not. The moment he would declare it to be a piece of junk, she would defend it as the most valuable piece of art Julius Eckert ever owned.

"Which is why, I suppose, it's been rotting out here in the garden for like a thousand years," he said aloud as he lifted the statue.

That's when the idea hit him. A simple exchange! He'd take the helmet from the suit of armor, attach it to a tall patio umbrella, stick it in the spot where the statue had been, and cover everything with vines and weeds. Then he'd hide the fountain statue in the basement under a blanket. He knew the expert on medieval armor was not due to visit Eckert House until next week. That would give Dan plenty of time to figure out how to fix the dented little angel. And it was an angel, for as Dan cleared away the vines that had hidden it for years, he saw a pair of wings in the back.

"Okay, Loretta, let's get you out of sight." For some reason, to Dan the angel looked as though it should be named Loretta. And so Loretta it was. He pushed Loretta to the house in a wheelbarrow and eased her down the stairs to the basement. Then he put Loretta in the darkest corner of room 8B and covered her with a moldy old quilt.

Then he went up to the Main Salon to move the suit of armor. "C'mon, Boris," he said as he hauled the suit of armor out of the Main Salon and took it to the basement. The suit of armor had always been Boris to him. He covered Boris with an old piece of canvas, then snuck Boris's helmet out of the house. After mounting the helmet on an old umbrella, Dan placed the umbrella in the exact spot where Loretta had stood. He did such a good job covering Boris's helmet and the umbrella with weeds and vines that when Dan was finished, it was tough to see it wasn't Loretta under all the leaves and vines.

As Dan walked back toward the house, he thought of his father and what he might think about all that had happened in the last few days. Dan was sure his dad would be proud that Dan was handling things on his own. He was sure that, as the Scripture said, he was growing in wisdom. But in that same moment another voice came to him — a voice that simply asked one question: "Are you sure?"

Dan stopped. *Was* he sure?

"I'll think about that later — when all this gets sorted out," he said, and he headed inside.

Mrs. Doheny was at her desk in the front hall. She was having an unpleasant conversation with a well-dressed little man with a bushy moustache.

"I'm sorry," she insisted, "but the museum is closed until Monday. You'll have to come back then."

"Don't you understand? I'm from *Yesterday's Architecture Today*. We're a very important magazine. I just need a few pictures of the gingerbread woodwork around the second-floor balcony."

The man had a whiny voice. Dan thought he was lucky he was talking to Mrs. Doheny. Miss Alma would have thrown him out without any discussion.

"Monday. Come back Monday. Please," said Mrs. Doheny, more pleading than forceful.

The man picked up his camera bag from her desk, looked at Dan as if he had something to do with not being able to take his pictures, and stormed out the front door.

"He just walked right in here. There's a Closed Until Further Notice sign right on the front door, and he just walked right in!" Mrs. Doheny dabbed her forehead with her handkerchief.

"It's like everyone's in a bad mood since—" Dan stopped himself. He almost said "since I discovered David Eckert's body." He couldn't let anybody in Eckert House know what he knew.

"Miss Alma would like to see you in her office.

Right away." Mrs. Doheny knew she was not giving Dan good news.

Dan nodded and climbed the stairs to the third floor. Miss Alma was on the phone when he knocked on the open door of her tiny office. She waved him in.

"You will refund all of the $53, and the check will be here by this time next week," she demanded. Then, without waiting for an answer, she hung up the phone. On his way up the stairs Dan had made sure that his hat was off, his shirt was tucked in, and that he was reasonably clean. He didn't want to give Miss Alma a reason to criticize him.

"Your shoe is untied," she informed him.

Dan sighed. He knelt down and tied his shoelace.

"Mr. Pruitt, would you say you are a curious young man?"

Dan saw that Miss Alma was watching him very closely. He straightened and chose his words with caution. Dan didn't know what she knew about his adventures, but she obviously knew something.

"Well, ma'am, I've been known to ask a lot of questions, if that's what you mean."

"Do you have any questions for me, Mr. Pruitt?"

Boy, did he ever. Like what did she mean when she said, "Let the dead rest in peace," and why was there a secret passageway in the house (and where else did it go), and why was there blood on the wall in the secret room, and why was "Davey" scratched on the floor, and . . . but would he get real answers? Especially if what he suspected was true, that Miss Alma was connected to the whole mystery.

"Well, ma'am," he finally answered, needing to say something, "since you asked, could I set the lawn mower to cut the grass at two inches instead of an inch and a half? I think some of the lawn will burn in this heat if it's cut too short."

Miss Alma looked at him as if he had just told her he was part of the first wave of an alien invasion that was coming to conquer earth.

"You may raise the blades of the lawn mower." She was not amused.

"Thank you, ma'am."

Dan started to leave, closing his eyes in relief as he headed for the door.

"That's not all, Mr. Pruitt," she called out.

Dan stopped. He was caught. He knew it. *Well*, he thought as he turned back to face her, *might as well stand here and take it like a man.*

"Yes, ma'am?"

"I have something for you." Dan had seen a movie once where a gangster said that very same thing to a guy named Jinks. *I have something for you.* Ten seconds later, Jinks was lying in a heap on the floor. Then again, Miss Alma didn't sound angry. If anything, she sounded . . . nice. That made Dan even more nervous. *She's toying with me,* Dan thought.

"You don't have to give me anything, Miss Alma," Dan offered, finally speaking up, hoping to avoid disaster.

"No, I don't. But I want to."

I'll bet, Dan thought. *Like two weeks in jail. That would get me out of the way so you could cover up whatever it is you don't want me to know.*

Miss Alma handed Dan a leather-bound diary. And he decided she really was being nice. Or so it seemed.

"This has been in our files for a number of years," she explained. "From what we can tell it's a diary kept by a boy whose father went off to fight in World War II. No one knows who wrote it or how it came to Eckert House. I'm fairly certain it was not written by anyone in the family. But that's just my opinion. I'd like you to take a look at it and see what you think. Interested?"

Dan was. Very interested! He took the book and flipped through the pages. The entries were written in the watery blue ink of a fountain pen. The boy's handwriting was much neater than Dan's own messy scrawl. Dan realized he had to say something to Miss Alma.

"Why are you giving this to me?" was the best he could do, and it came out before he could stop himself. The corners of Miss Alma's mouth twitched and almost looked as if they were forming a tiny smile.

"I have my reasons," she answered. "Being a boy, which I am not, you might have more insights into what kind of a young man he was. I would very much like to learn his identity. And there's something else. I believe you are one of those young people who need to have something that is yours and yours alone. I have known other boys like you. One in particular . . . " Her voice trailed off. Then, aware that Dan was watching her closely, she shook her head as if to erase a memory and looked back at him. "This, Mr. Pruitt, is just for you. Do you accept?"

"You bet," Dan said.

There was a faint hint of a smile on Miss Alma's face, but Dan missed it this time. She gave him instructions on how to care for the book and keep it from harm. Then she sent him on his way.

But before he got to the door, she said, "Eckert House has too many secrets. I don't like secrets, Mr. Pruitt."

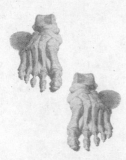

THE DIARY

"I think she does know—at least I think she knows you were in the secret passageway," Shelby said after listening to Dan's entire story without saying a word.

Dan, Shelby, and Pete had gathered in the tree so Dan could tell them about all that he had discovered at Eckert House the day before and show them the diary Miss Alma had given him.

"Why didn't she bust me then?"

"Too dangerous," Shelby said. "The last thing Miss Alma wants is for you to keep poking around and asking questions about David Eckert." She held up the diary. "That's why she gave you this. To throw you off track."

This drew blank looks from Dan and Pete.

"C'mon, you guys. Don't be dense. This is exactly what the bad guy does in the movies. He sends the hero off on a wild-goose chase so he can steal the money or get rid of the witness or get out of town."

"So tell me, Search Engine," Dan said with a smile, "are you saying I'm a hero?"

"In your dreams. And stop calling me Search Engine or I'm gonna come up with a nickname for you."

"You mean like 'Hero'?" he persisted.

"I was thinking more along the lines of 'Pasta Head.'"

Pete laughed. It was typical of Dan and Shelby to exchange insults, but he never felt comfortable enough to join in.

It was Shelby's opinion that the diary, while interesting, was worthless.

"Why would she give it to you if it was valuable?"

Dan had to agree.

"Still, she seemed sincere," he added.

"Of course she did. That's all part of her game." Once Shelby made up her mind about something, she rarely changed it. And she had made up her mind about Miss Alma and her involvement in the mystery.

Shelby wanted to hear all about the secret passageway again, and she made Dan tell it to her from the beginning. Pete picked up the diary and started to read, tuning out Dan and Shelby as he turned page after page. He ignored them as they speculated about how many other secret rooms there might be in Eckert House.

"Hey, Dan, listen to this! It's from May 1943." Pete found the spot and started reading. "'I miss my father and wish he would write. I guess Hitler and his gang are keeping him busy over there. Before he left, Pop told me not to worry, and I wish I could take his advice, but it's tough.'" Pete lowered the diary. "That's almost exactly what you said a few days ago about your dad. Remember?"

Dan didn't say a word. He just took the diary from Pete and closed it.

"Sorry," Pete said.

"No big deal."

But it was. Pete and Shelby both understood how much Dan worried about his father. Shelby decided a change of subject was needed.

"Hey, did I tell you what I found outside my front door this morning? Is this weird or what? I found a dead bird with a ribbon twisted around its neck. The ribbon must have been hanging on a branch or something, and the bird got caught on it." Shelby looked at Pete. He looked scared. "What's wrong?"

"There was a dead bird with a ribbon around its neck on *my* front steps this morning," he whispered.

"Very funny," she shot back. "Here something interesting finally happens to me and you make a joke out of it."

"I . . . I . . . I'm not kidding," Pete stammered.

"Seriously?" she asked.

"Seriously."

Shelby believed Pete. He was not the kind of guy who would lie. About anything.

Both Pete and Shelby looked at Dan.

"There wasn't a dead bird outside my door," Dan said. "And before you both get all goofy on me, let me point out that you each have a cat, and cats like to bring dead birds and animals home. It's just something they do. Especially that bizarre cat of yours." He looked right at Shelby. "Didn't Rigoletto capture a woodchuck once?"

"Yes, but he didn't put a nice big bow on it and then ring my doorbell!"

"Is that what happened with the bird?" Dan asked.

"Someone rang the doorbell and there it was, all wrapped up like a birthday present?"

"Why are you acting like this?" Shelby demanded.

Dan knew exactly why he was acting this way: He suspected that the same person who had sent him the picture and the threatening note had given the dead birds to Pete and Shelby. Dan was scared. He was scared because it felt like *he* was getting another warning. Dan didn't want to say anything to his friends ... yet. He needed time to figure out what to do.

65

"Look," he said, "this has gotta be a gag. Maybe it's Jesse and Dylan. Isn't this the kind of thing they'd do?"

Pete and Shelby agreed that it was.

"My advice, then, is to ignore it. They just want to get some kind of reaction out of you. Don't give it to them."

Dan hoped that by saying this he could keep Shelby and Pete away from Jesse and Dylan. That way his fake story blaming the twins wouldn't be exposed.

"I wouldn't give them the time of day," Shelby declared.

"The last thing I want is Jesse and Dylan thinking they scared me," Pete added.

Dan told Pete and Shelby that he was going back to Eckert House to continue his search. He planned to check the family history and the files that were kept in a special room on the third floor. "Miss Alma may have given me this diary to throw me off the track—"

"*Did* give you the diary to throw you off track," insisted Shelby.

"Okay, okay. But I'm gonna use it as an excuse to research the Eckert family and find out more about David Eckert. And I'm gonna do it right under Miss

Alma's nose."

Shelby decided she would go to the library to see if she could find out anything about the person who disappeared around the time that David Eckert was supposed to have committed a murder.

"The rumor never much interested me before, but now it does," she said. "Let me see what I can find out. Sometimes what a newspaper *doesn't* say is just as interesting as what it does." She took off in the direction of the library.

Pete walked with Dan down the hill toward Eckert House. Something was bothering him.

"This diary...," Pete started. But he didn't finish.

"C'mon, spill it." Dan was anxious to go into the museum and get started.

"I'm kinda wondering if . . . well, if there's another reason Miss Alma gave it to you."

"Like?"

"Like maybe what's written inside . . . the way that other boy felt . . . maybe she wants you to read *that*."

Dan stopped.

"You mean you think she's on the level?"

"She could be. That boy's dad was gone, yours is gone, his dad flew airplanes, so does yours, he was scared, and I think you are too. Isn't it possible that she's trying to help you in some way . . . that's she's being nice? I know she can be a pain, but why can't we think the best of her?"

Why not think the best of Miss Alma? Well, thought Dan, someone sent the birds as a warning, and his best guess was that she did it. But he couldn't say that to his cousin. Or to Shelby. Or to anybody. Not yet, anyway. Not until he knew more. For now, though, he had to give Pete some kind of answer.

"I promise to try and see it from her point of view," Dan said. *In other words,* he said to himself, *I'll try to think like a criminal.*

"One more thing," Pete said, as Dan was about to step through the front gate of Eckert House, "if you ever need to just talk, if stuff's bothering you, let me know."

"Thanks, I will." But Dan knew his answer was too quick. Pete probably realized Dan didn't really mean it.

As Dan disappeared through the front door of Eckert House, Pete whispered, "Please take care of him, Lord. I'm not sure he knows how much he needs you."

THE STORM

"You lost a very important letter," Miss Alma snapped at Mrs. Doheny just as Dan walked in the door.

"I'm sorry. I know I'll find it," Mrs. Doheny promised.

"See that you do." Miss Alma then turned to Dan, a letter in her outstretched hand. "This came for you, Mr. Pruitt. Have you listed this as your official address now?" Then, without waiting for an answer, she said, "Please don't," and walked away.

Mrs. Doheny wiped away a tear.

"What did you lose?" Dan whispered.

The letter, Mrs. Doheny explained, was from a man coming from Germany to authenticate, and possibly buy, the suit of armor. "Now Miss Alma wants to postpone the visit, but neither of us can remember his name or the name of the company he represents. I just don't understand what could have happened to it," she mumbled as she shuffled through the papers on her desk.

Dan suddenly had bigger things to worry about.

He opened and stared at the letter Miss Alma had given him. It was just two sentences. "So, now you know. I'm warning you, don't get in my way." Dan quickly folded the letter and shoved it, and the envelope, into his pocket. His heart was thumping wildly. He needed some time to calm down, to think, so he walked into the library and ducked behind a bookcase. He pulled the envelope out to see if there was a postmark. There was none. Just like the other letter that had been put in his mailbox, the stamp in the upper right corner had not been canceled.

Dan looked up from the letter. In front of him was the strange photograph of the party where everyone was dressed as Sherlock Holmes.

"What would you make of all this?" he asked the

"Sherlock Holmes" in the center of the picture, the one who seemed to be in charge of the party, the one the framed invitation said would lead everyone to a "whopping body of evidence."

Instinctively, Dan knew the answer. There was a body of evidence he had to follow, and he couldn't be afraid of it. Dan walked back out to Mrs. Doheny's desk.

"Who delivered the mail today?" he asked.

"The same person as usual, you know, that nice-looking, tall man," she answered.

"Did he hand it right to you?"

"No, he put it in the tray right over there, like he always does. I remember, because I was just going to get a cup of tea when he walked in."

"Then you picked up the mail when you came back?" Dan asked.

"No, it was gone."

"How long were you gone?"

"Oh, five, maybe ten minutes. But turns out Miss Alma took the mail while I was gone."

"What did Miss Alma do with it?"

"As a matter of fact, she took it upstairs. She came back down with it right after I had gotten back to my desk. She said she had forgotten she had it. But I remember thinking that was strange, because Miss Alma never forgets anything."

No, thought Dan, *she doesn't. And by going upstairs, she had plenty of time to slip my letter in with the others.*

"Thanks," he said, and headed up the stairway to the third floor, to Miss Alma's office. "Don't get in my way," the letter said. *Don't worry, Miss Alma,* Dan thought, *I won't get in your way. I'll stay three steps ahead of you.*

Once upstairs, Dan explained to Miss Alma that he wanted to make absolutely sure that the writer of the diary was not an Eckert. He was sincere about that, for he did want to exclude any Eckerts as possible authors of the journal. But he really wanted to look through the family files and find out what they said about David Eckert.

Miss Alma gave him permission to do his research in the little room next to her office where the files were kept.

"That's excellent critical thinking, Mr. Pruitt," she said as she unlocked the door of the little room. If she suspected anything, she didn't let on.

A storm had been brewing all morning, and now, as Dan sat down to search for clues about David Eckert, the first raindrops splattered against the tiny round window high on the wall above him.

Dan pulled out volumes of birth certificates, death certificates, marriage licenses, and other official documents. He was soon lost in all the details of the Eckert family. He felt the way he often did when he was reading a good book — that he was caught up in another world.

There were six different David Eckerts. All were first sons. The first David Eckert was the saintly older brother of Julius Eckert. While Julius circled the globe collecting objects of interest, the first David Eckert circled the globe as a missionary doctor helping the sick.

The next three David Eckerts were all born in the 1800s, so Dan didn't pay any attention to them, although he did pause to read a newspaper account of how the third David Eckert stopped a riot in Freemont just after the start of the Spanish-American War. From what Dan could figure out, people in the town were convinced that the Spanish navy had sailed up the Morgan River and was about to attack the village. The fact that battleships from Spain could not have gotten into Pennsylvania was something that apparently did not occur to anyone except David Eckert. After calming the mob down, he sent them all home to bed.

The fifth David Eckert was born in 1901, and the sixth David Eckert—the last known David Eckert—was born in 1938. Neither could have been the teenager who supposedly killed someone and then was killed in 1943. One was too old and the other was too young. Besides, records clearly showed that Number Five died in 1956, and Number Six moved to Florida with his parents in 1942, when he was only four years old.

"This doesn't make any sense," muttered Dan. "None of these David Eckerts could have done it." And yet he knew that something had happened. He had found a skeleton in the garden and had a threatening letter in his pocket.

"What would Search Engine do?" he wondered aloud. "Tell me not to call her that, first. Then she'd have a creative way to double-check her facts."

Dan wondered what other ways there might be to check if someone else lived at Eckert House. Other records.

"One thing's for sure," Dan mumbled, "if the guy I want to find was born here in this house, then his birth certificate has been intentionally removed by someone."

A loud clap of thunder made Dan jump and he automatically said, "I'm listening." That was a family joke. Whenever Grandpa Mike heard thunder, he would say that God was trying to get his attention, and he always called out, "I'm listening!"

Thinking about God getting his attention got Dan to think about church, and church got Dan to thinking about one church in particular—Holy Apostles, the congregation where the Eckerts had always worshiped. In fact the large brick structure at Freemont's four corners, where the town first started, had been built mostly with Eckert money. The Eckerts were very big churchgoers, and the joke was that every one of them had been "hatched, matched, and dispatched" out of Holy Apostles. Dan knew that "hatched" meant baptized, "matched" meant married, and "dispatched" meant funerals. He also realized that churches kept records of all those events.

"Well," said Dan quietly, for he found that it helped him think if he spoke out loud, "the David Eckert I'm looking for was buried out by the fountain, so there sure wasn't an official funeral for him. And if he was locked in the tower, then there's no way he ever got married. But when he was born they didn't know he was going to have problems, so he would have been baptized! There's got to be a record! Search Engine, you'd be proud of me!"

In a flash Dan was on his feet looking for the volume that contained all the baptismal certificates. He located it, pulled the dusty book off the shelf, and started looking for the proof. If the stories were true, this David Eckert would have been eighteen in 1943. That meant he would have been baptized around 1925. A few minutes later, he found the baptismal certificate.

The certificate, preserved in plastic, was from 1925 — July 18, 1925, to be exact. And it clearly stated in a very fancy but spidery handwriting that David James Eckert, son of Bernard and Florence Eckert, was baptized on that day. Whoever had destroyed his birth certificate had forgotten about the elegant little piece of paper recording his baptism.

Dan now had no doubt that David Eckert, *his* David Eckert, was real. But the strangest thing of all was that his parents, Bernard and Florence, were also the parents of the David Eckert who was born in 1938, when *his* David would have been thirteen.

Why would they do that? Dan wondered. He could think of only one reason. The original David was strange in some way, and the family wanted a different David—a "better" one. So they took the first son's name, a name which had been handed down from generation to generation, and gave it to the next son. The cruelty of such an action made Dan's face flush with anger.

Now the storm was directly overhead. A bright flash of lightning and the loudest clap of thunder Dan had ever heard plunged Eckert House into darkness. The power was out.

Dan jumped up and crossed to the door. It was only late afternoon, but the darkness of the clouds overhead, combined with the total lack of any light inside, made the museum quite gloomy.

"Of all the inconsiderate things," Miss Alma complained. "Mr. Pruitt!"

"Right here, ma'am," Dan called out as he stumbled to her office.

The emergency lights mounted high on the wall at each end of the hall flickered on.

"Come with me," Miss Alma said. "The backup generator has not kicked on yet, and if it doesn't within the next few minutes, I have to switch our alarm system over to the auxiliary power. I need you to come down to the basement with me and help reset it."

"But, Miss Alma, I don't know anything about alarm systems!" Dan declared.

"Do you know how to hold a flashlight?" she asked rather sharply.

"Yes, ma'am."

"Then come with me."

Resetting the alarm system was a matter of pressing the right buttons in the proper sequence. The control panel was in a little room near the bottom of the basement stairs. Dan held the flashlight, but Miss Alma made him turn his head so he could not see what the numbers were for the alarm system.

"There," she said. "Now, if that other generator would just behave itself, then we—" She suddenly stopped. She was looking at a spot behind Dan, peering into the darkness.

"Miss Alma?" Dan said, slightly worried.

"Quiet!" she whispered. They both stood very still.

"Who's there?" she called out.

Now Dan heard what she had heard, a sort of shuffling at the far end of the basement. Miss Alma turned off the flashlight, plunging them into total darkness. Dan felt her brush past him. She vanished into the inky blackness.

No one knew Eckert House as well as Miss Alma

did. Now she used that knowledge as she crept silently forward to confront whatever, or whoever, was out there in the darkness. Dan knew better than to call after her. The fear he had of what or who was down in that basement with them kept him rooted to the same spot for a long time. He heard nothing. Finally he thought he could steal to the bottom of the stairs without making any noise and go for help.

Just as Dan reached the bottom step, he heard a loud bang, almost as if someone had slammed a door. Miss Alma let out a cry of alarm. Dan didn't know what to do. Should he rush upstairs and get help or try to feel his way through the darkness toward Miss Alma? He called her name. She didn't answer. Then he saw the beam from her flashlight.

"Mr. Pruitt!" she called.

As Dan was running toward her, the lights came back on. The power had been restored.

Miss Alma was lying on the floor. A large box was open, on its side, right next to her.

"Are you okay? What happened? Who was down here? How did he get out? Did he throw this box at you?" Dan fired all this at Miss Alma as he helped her to her feet.

"I'm fine." She sighed as she tried to brush dust off her dress. "And this is not a press conference, Mr. Pruitt. I have nothing else to say." And she didn't. But as they walked back toward the stairs, and as Miss Alma looked nervously around the room, Dan got the feeling that there was a lot she could say. She just wasn't going to say it to him.

The rain had slowed, and Miss Alma sent Dan outside to check all the electrical lines leading to the museum. He was to make sure that no branches had fallen onto any of them. All the lines were clear, but as Dan crossed the lawn, something caught his eye. Near the fountain, a piece of ribbon was snagged on a bush and fluttered in the wind. He walked toward it and thought of Shelby and Pete and the ribbons they had found twisted around the necks of the dead birds that had been left on their porches.

Dan approached the fountain cautiously. He stopped at the edge of the hole where he had found the skeleton. The hole was now almost filled with rainwater, and in the water, face down, was the helmet from the suit of armor. Dan picked up the helmet. Attached to its visor was a ribbon with a note. The paper was soaked, but the words written on it were still legible: "You're next," the note read.

THE CLUES

Dan had a very bad night. The afternoon storm that had cut power to the area was followed by another storm around nine o'clock, and still another after midnight. The rumbling thunder and flashes of lightning only added to his anxiety. One ka-boom of thunder was so loud he sat up in bed and, just as he had that afternoon, said, "I'm listening."

Are you sure?

There it was again. That small voice that Dan had tried to ignore. He knew then that he had not been listening to God, and now, at 1:35 in the morning, he was wide awake because of it.

"And Jesus grew in wisdom and in stature, and in favor with God and men."

Dan took out his Bible, turned to the gospel of Luke, and even though he knew the verse by heart, he read it again. It always made him feel closer to his father when he did. After reading the word "wisdom," Dan had to admit that some of the decisions he had made lately were anything but wise. He had kept secrets, he had lied, he had put his friends in danger, he had said he was doing one thing while he actually did another, he had damaged property and then covered it up, he had made himself look important. The list went on and on.

"Not a great week, Dan," he said out loud. "And the thing is, you knew you were making bad choices." He made a prayerful promise to come clean with Pete and Shelby the next day. Only then was he able to fall back to sleep.

"Okay, let's go over what we have," Shelby said. Shelby, Dan, and Pete were sitting around Pete's kitchen table eating lunch.

"Wait a minute," Dan said. "I just told you what I had done. Aren't you mad at me?"

"No," she said.

"You said you were sorry," Pete added.

"But I knew you guys were in danger and I didn't tell you!"

"Which only proves that your first impulse was to be a dope, and afterwards you thought better of it," Shelby answered. "We understand. Let's move on."

"Uh . . . thanks," Dan said.

"You're welcome," said Shelby. "Right now we have to figure out what to do next."

She was right. Before Dan could go to Miss Alma to apologize, they had to decide if she was part of the problem. If she was, Dan was going straight to the police.

Dan suggested they write all the evidence they had gathered on slips of paper and lay them on the table to see if there was some kind of pattern. "First things first. David Eckert, fact or fiction?" He wrote the name on a piece of paper.

"Fact," said Shelby.

"Fact," echoed Pete.

"Fact," agreed Dan.

"Supporting evidence?" Shelby asked.

Dan repeated the story of the baptismal certificate he had found and said he had seen the name "Davey" scratched in the floor of the tower room.

"Then there's the little matter of his bones," he added.

"Which, technically speaking, we don't know are his," Pete reminded them.

"Good point," Shelby agreed. "But I think we can say with some certainty that David Eckert was real."

"And that something was wrong with him," Dan said, surprising both Shelby and Pete. "Listen to this." He pulled out the diary. "It's from 1941. April 6. I found it last night." Dan read:

I saw him again. Someone hit the ball across the street and over the fence. I ran after it. He was up there in the window, and he was watching. He waved at me and I waved back. He looked so lonely. I remember him from before. I was only six, but I remember. Sometimes the nurses brought him over to the park. They let me talk to him. Mother didn't. She grabbed me and pulled me away when she saw who it was. She told me I was never to do that again. What did she call him? Was it a Chinaman? Why did she not want me to talk to someone from China?

Dan closed the diary. "He was writing about David Eckert. I'm sure of it. See, a ball hit from the open space in the park, the spot where the kids in Freemont have always played baseball, would enter the Eckert House property to the north of the house. Someone chasing it would have a good view of the little tower that was hidden from the street by the big chimney." Dan jotted some notes down on a slip of paper. "I believe David Eckert was locked in that tower, and there *was* something wrong with him." Dan tapped the journal with his finger. "The way this boy's mother reacted proves it."

"What if the mother was prejudiced? What if this boy was from China or Korea or something and the mother just didn't want her son near him?" This came from Pete.

"Of course that's possible," Dan agreed. "But why was he there with nurses? It doesn't say 'nanny' or 'governess' or 'baby-sitter.' It says 'nurses.' Plural."

Shelby didn't have a problem with any of Dan's information about David Eckert. In fact, if Dan had been paying close attention to her, he would have seen that she already seemed to know all about David Eckert. After some discussion, even Pete had to agree that the evidence pointed toward the probability that, for some reason, David Eckert needed constant supervision.

The next question was what, if anything, happened in 1943, the year David Eckert mysteriously disappeared? Shelby had done a lot of research.

"But if you start calling me Search Engine," she warned Dan, "I'm going home."

Dan nodded.

By reading old newspaper accounts and talking to Mr. Griffith, the town's ancient librarian, and his sister, Eleanor, Shelby had pieced together the following story:

"In 1943, there was a family, the Martinis. Their son, Mario, worked for the Eckerts. Kind of like you do, Dan. He was only sixteen. So was Ethel Eckert, a cousin visiting from Savannah. That's a point you'll want to remember. There were Eckert cousins all over the country, and whenever one of the Eckerts came for a visit, it always made the society page of the paper — written by Miriam Eckert, a sister-in-law to Hollis Eckert, David Eckert's grandfather. So here we go.

Fact: Ethel, who was supposed to stay here in Freemont until September, returned to Georgia by train in August, August 1st according to the society page of the August 8th paper.

Fact: Ethel Eckert couldn't have left on the 1st because it was a Sunday, and back then the train didn't come through Freemont on Sundays.

Fact: Mr. Griffith and his sister both saw Ethel Eckert at the train station August 7th leaving Freemont.

Fact: In that same society column on August 8th, Mario Martini was reported as being in Pittsburgh at the baseball game with the Boy Scouts the night of August 5th.

Fact: That was impossible, because the Pirates were not even playing in town on August 5, 1943.

Fact: As the son of Italian immigrants, Mario Martini was never mentioned before or after in the society page.

Fact: There was a fire at Eckert House on August 5th.

Fact: An ambulance went to Eckert House the night of the fire, but no injuries were reported in the paper.

Fact: Mario Martini was elected president of his high school class at the end of his junior year, June 1943.

Fact: Mario Martini never returned to Freemont High School in the fall of 1943, and Shirley Hallock was named class president.

Fact: Guess who was at Eckert House when all of this happened? C'mon, guess!"

Dan and Pete stared at Shelby. She had just bombarded them with a ton of information, none of which made much sense, and now she wanted them to answer a riddle.

"One of the nurse's aides was a young woman named Alma Louise Stockton LeMay."

"What!"

"Miss Alma?"

"Mr. Griffith and his sister remember her well. She was as much of a pain then as she is now. She never told anyone who she worked for at Eckert House or why she was even there. But she was. And she left with Ethel Eckert . . . on the same train."

Shelby wrote the names Ethel Eckert, Mario Martini, and Miss Alma on slips of paper and placed them on the table. Then she began to explain her conclusions.

"There is a very strong case to be made that Ethel Eckert and Mario Martini fell in love. And that her family disapproved. You know the story, the same old, same old. He was a poor boy from the wrong side of the tracks, they were a distinguished family, blah, blah, blah. And who knows, maybe things would have eventually worked out. After all, there was a war on, and a lot of people got married under unusual circumstances. But things got complicated, and I think it was because of David Eckert.

"After August 5, Mario Martini disappeared, never to be heard from again. Right around that same time, as the rumors tell it, David Eckert died.

"On August 7, 1943, Miss Alma and Ethel Eckert travel by train to Savannah. Miss Alma didn't return to Freemont until 1956.

"Conclusion: I think Mario Martini was killed by David Eckert on August 5 for reasons that may well have had to do with Mario falling in love with Ethel. I think the story about Mario being at the baseball game was made up to 'prove' that he was somewhere else. I think the fire at the house was real, but it was a cover-up. I think it was set intentionally after Mario's father heard what had happened, and he came over to Eckert House and killed David Eckert. I think Ethel Eckert was so upset that Miss Alma was paid by the family to get her out of town and take her back to her home."

Dan and Pete sat in silence. Shelby watched them. Finally Dan said, "Most of that makes sense, but you're leaving out one very big possibility."

"What?" Shelby demanded.

"How old was Miss Alma when all this happened?"

"Eighteen or so. Very young. Why?"

"I believe," Dan said, speaking very slowly, "that she was much more involved in this than you suppose. If she's the one sending the notes, and I think she is, then she has something to hide."

"But what?"

Dan thought about what Miss Alma had said when she gave him the diary, "I have known other boys like you. One in particular."

There had been a faraway look in her eyes when she'd said it. Suddenly Dan was sure he knew what she meant.

"Miss Alma was in love with Mario Martini," Dan

said. "She killed him when she discovered he loved Ethel Eckert instead. Who knows, maybe it was even an accident. But she let Mario's father think David Eckert had killed his son. The Eckerts didn't want any scandal. Miss Alma made her escape when the family paid her to get Ethel out of town." Dan took a deep breath. "We need to go to the police and tell them everything we know."

Pete and Shelby agreed. They started gathering up all of their notes.

"Hey, can you guys wait a few minutes?" Pete asked. "Our next-door neighbor is on vacation and I'm taking care of her dog. I have to feed it before we go."

"Sure," Dan said. He didn't mind waiting. He knew going to the police would be tough. The police were going to ask why, when he got the first note, he hadn't reported it, and he didn't have a good answer.

"Just think," Shelby said, "Miss Alma almost got away with murder."

Dan said it was her own fault that she was getting caught after all these years. "If she hadn't made me dig up that tree, the body would have stayed hidden."

"Why is Pete letting that horrible dog bark so much?" Shelby asked in an annoyed tone. "Do you think Chester's bothering him?"

"That cat wouldn't bother with a little thing like a dog when he can sprawl out in the street and scare big things like cars," Dan said.

They went out the back door and looked into the yard next door. The dog was running in circles, barking frantically. But they didn't see Pete. Then they saw that the neighbor's back door was standing wide open. Something was wrong.

"Pete?" Dan called as he and Shelby ran into the neighbor's yard.

"Pete!"

They searched the neighbor's yard and house, calling to Pete, but he never answered.

Pete was gone.

"We have to call the police and get them over to Eckert House," Dan cried after several minutes of growing panic. "Miss Alma's at it again. She's grabbed Pete!"

THE CHASE

That afternoon, for the second time in less than two weeks, the police descended on Eckert House. Their conversation with Miss Alma did not go well.

"You don't understand! This is the exact wrong time for you to be here!" Miss Alma seemed more frantic than angry.

"The element of surprise is a policeman's best friend," Sergeant Haines said.

"*Your* best friend," she scoffed, "is the dimwit who gives you a paycheck every week."

As Sergeant Haines escorted Miss Alma down the hall, Dan and Shelby, who had snuck in right after the police, backed against the wall. It didn't help. Miss Alma saw them. She was surprisingly calm. Dan hoped she didn't realize that he and Shelby were the ones who had reported her to the police.

"I once asked you if you had any questions, Mr. Pruitt. It's a pity you didn't ask them."

"I . . . I . . . I . . ." But Dan couldn't utter another word.

Then, looking Dan right in the eye, she said, "There's no worse lie than a misunderstood truth."

Sergeant Haines touched Miss Alma's elbow and they moved toward the front door. She stopped after a few steps and turned back.

"Keep your eyes open, Mr. Pruitt."

A moment later, she was gone.

"Can you believe that?" Shelby said. "She threatened you right in front of the police! Well, that's the end of her." She sighed with relief.

A strange feeling came over Dan, a feeling that he had made a terrible mistake, a feeling that Miss Alma's words to keep his eyes open were meant as advice and a warning, not as a threat.

Mrs. Doheny came out of the Little Salon. With her was a bald-headed gentleman. He was well dressed and carried an elegant walking stick with a gold band near the top.

"I'll just get Miss Alma," she said to him. Then she giggled. Whoever he was, he certainly had Mrs. Doheny acting like a teenager.

"Miss Alma is—" Shelby started to say, but Dan stopped her.

"Miss Alma will be right back," he said loudly. Shelby looked at him, wondering what was wrong. Dan was studying the man intently.

"Well, then, Baron Von Siegler," Mrs. Doheny gushed, "if you'll just have a seat in the Main Salon, I'll bring you that tea." She turned to Dan and Shelby. "The baron is here about the suit of armor. Keep him company for a minute, please." She hurried back to the kitchen, obviously not wanting her important guest to wait one moment longer than necessary for his tea.

On a normal day, the appearance of the baron might have worried Dan. After all, he had come all the way from Germany to possibly buy Boris, and Boris was currently in two pieces; the body armor was down in the basement, and the helmet was rusting away out in the toolshed. Dan was trying to figure out how to reunite Boris with his head, when he stopped. Something about the way the baron turned and walked away reminded him of someone else, someone he had seen in that exact spot very recently. Of course! The photographer from the magazine! It was the same man!

Miss Alma knew it, too. Not about the photographer, but about this man. She somehow knew he was a fake. That's what she had been trying to tell Dan as she was taken away. Keep your eyes open, she said. Well, Dan's eyes were opened now. He knew something else, too. He knew he had been wrong about a lot of things at Eckert House. He now wondered just how this strange man was involved in the mystery.

Instead of going into the Main Salon, as Mrs. Doheny had suggested, the Baron wandered into the library.

Dan turned to Shelby. His voice was low, but his tone was intense.

"I need you to listen to me. Without being obvious, look outside and tell me if there's a strange car out front."

She walked over to the window. "There is — a mini-van with no windows in either its back or its sides. It's backed up toward the house."

"Okay, now, no questions. When we came in, Jesse and Dylan and a bunch of the guys were across the street in the park. Get them. And get every bike, scooter, and skateboard around. Wait at the park entrance, but try not to be obvious. Go."

The urgent tone in Dan's voice erased any thought Shelby might have had about arguing with him. She walked out of the museum trying to think of what she was going to say to the guys in the park, but she knew that somehow she'd get them to do what Dan asked.

Dan walked up to "Baron Von Siegler" in the library. The man was looking at the picture of the party where everyone had dressed as Sherlock Holmes.

"How fascinating to have so much time and money on your hands that you can throw a silly party like that," the man said in a slight German accent, an accent that Dan knew was fake. The baron used his walking stick to point at the invitation next to the photograph. "My grandfather was born on this same date in 1901. He began life as a very poor man, but my family rose to greatness."

Dan didn't know what to say. He just knew he had to keep the man occupied for a few minutes. He started talking about the one thing the man was supposedly interested in. "And now you're here to buy a tin can that someone once walked around in."

As he said it, Dan remembered something else. It was right after this man came in pretending to be a photographer that the letter from the German collector disappeared from Mrs. Doheny's desk. The man had been standing right in front of the desk. Dan was sure "the photographer" had taken the letter that afternoon and used the information to pretend to be "the Baron."

But why? Obviously to get something. But what?

Dan kept the baron talking about his castle in Bavaria to give himself time to think. One thing Dan knew for sure was that the little bald-headed man was not after Boris. Boris, because of what Dan did to him, was probably worth a fraction of his value. That, and denting the little angel were something Dan would have to come clean about when Miss Alma got back. Especially if, as he was beginning to suspect, Miss Alma was not the villain he thought she was.

That's when it hit Dan. That's when he figured it out. He literally slapped his head with his hand.

"You are such a loser!" he cried.

The baron stopped in mid-sentence and looked at Dan. "I beg your pardon?" he said.

"Excuse me," Dan called over his shoulder as he hurried out of the library.

Dan raced down the hall toward the open front door. The minivan was still parked out front. A man was loading a long object wrapped in an old quilt into the back of the vehicle. Already in the minivan was another object, wrapped in a blanket. This object rolled a little, all on its own, and Dan was sure he had found Pete.

Dan saw that Shelby was standing across the street with Jesse, Dylan, and a few others, at the entrance to the park.

When Dan turned around, he came face to face with the baron, who swung his walking stick like a baseball bat and bashed Dan on the side of the head. Dan's knees buckled from the sharp pain, and a wave of dizziness swept over him. He didn't black out, though. He forced himself to stand up, but he was too late to grab the little bald man as he fled to the waiting minivan.

Dan wasn't quite sure what instinct prompted him to grab the velvet rope hanging from hooks on brass poles that kept visitors from getting too close to the painting near the front door. He might have had some strange notion of using the rope as a weapon. But whatever the reason, he looked very odd as he staggered out of Eckert House, blood streaming down his face, swinging the velvet rope like a stubby lasso.

"Stop the van!" he yelled. "Stop the van! Pete is inside!"

Just then Mrs. Doheny came out on the porch with a teapot.

"Yoo-hoo! Baron! Do you want lemon or milk in your tea?" she called out in a high, giggly voice.

Jesse and Dylan were on their bikes and got to the minivan first. The baron had already jumped into the passenger seat and, dropping all trace of his German accent, told the driver to hit the gas.

The minivan started forward, but the sudden appearance of Jesse and Dylan caused the driver to slam on the brakes.

"Run them over if you have to!" the bald-headed man bellowed. The minivan jerked forward and Jesse and Dylan swerved out of the way. The delay gave Dan enough time to reach the van, jump on the skateboard Shelby had ready for him, and hook the velvet rope onto a trailer hitch on the back bumper.

"Everyone on a skateboard or scooter, grab on to me!" Dan called out as the van began to pull out into the street. Riley Addison and Ted Jamison, each on a skateboard, latched on to Dan's belt, one on the left, one on the right. Shelby, on a scooter, grabbed Riley's waistband, and Brandon Coles, on inline skates, grabbed Ted. They looked like a fighter squadron fanned out in a "V" formation.

The van picked up speed as it headed north on Golden Street. Jesse and Dylan easily kept pace on their bikes, hooting and hollering to get someone to call the police. As an extra touch, Jesse sang the theme song to his favorite superhero cartoon show.

The driver was unaware of the extra passengers until he turned right on Hulbert Avenue and headed up the steep hill. That's when he saw them in his rearview mirror.

"We got stowaways," he told the bald-headed man.

"Stowaways would be *inside* the van, you dolt!"

"Well, we got *something*. Any suggestions?"

The bald-headed man looked in his rearview mirror. "Speed up! Lose them!" he shouted.

As the minivan sped up, Dan saw Jesse and Dylan drop back. He looked over his shoulder and realized they were having a hard time pedaling up the steep hill.

"Jesse! Dylan! Get help! The police! Anybody! Tell them they have Pete!"

Still singing the theme song, Jesse and Dylan peeled off.

At the top of the hill, Hulbert crossed Church Street. If the van turned to the left, they would head into town. If it went straight ahead, they would continue up another short hill that circled Freemont's cemetery. If it turned to the right, they would head toward the bridge that crossed the Morgan River. The van went straight, not bothering to stop at the stop sign. Cars to the left and to the right on Church Street screeched to a halt as the minivan rolled through. No one in the cars expected to see it towing five children, much less to have one of them, Ted, give them a jaunty little wave as he whizzed past, but that's what happened.

"How are we doing?" Dan shouted.

"OK!" came back as a chorus. Everyone had managed to hold on, but the close call at the intersection had their hearts pumping fast and hard.

"What's your plan?" Riley yelled.

"I'm working on it!"

"Let us know when you come up with something!" Riley yelled back.

The driver realized he'd made a mistake as soon as he crested the hill and saw the cemetery smack in front of him. The cemetery itself was about the size of a football field, and the road that circled it was like the running tracks that circle many high school fields. This gave the bald-headed man an idea.

"Drive as fast as you can—three times around," he ordered. "Floor it!" Then he started to laugh. "We'll see how the little brats like this."

As they rounded the far curve, tires squealing, Dan knew what the men were trying to do. All five children swung wildly to the right. Brandon was the first to go. The force of the turn was too much for him and he sailed out over the grassy embankment. He was airborne for a full three seconds, and while those three seconds were thrilling and he let out a laugh of pure joy, his landing wasn't. Neither were the somersaults that took him down the steep hill and into some rosebushes. That part was just plain painful. However, when he stood up all battered, bloody, and torn, he realized he kind of looked like an action hero at the end of a movie.

Shelby was next. Try as she might to hold on to Riley, she was no match for centrifugal force. She and the scooter and, unfortunately, Ted (for she clipped him as she went flying) ended up in a heap in the grass around the fourth and fastest turn the van made.

"We got two that time," the driver cackled.

"Make sure you get the last two on this next turn."

The van increased its speed and, try as he might, Riley could not hold on.

"Sorry!" he yelled as he, too, somersaulted across a wide patch of soft grass. He rolled over and promptly threw up. Riley was never at his best going in circles. Even the merry-go-round at the fair made him sick.

"No problem!" Dan yelled. *No problem! Have you lost your mind?*

Shelby, as always, was in full control of her mind and she had scrambled to her feet and was picking up green apples that had fallen from the tree arching over her. She told Ted to do the same. She stepped as far out into the road as she dared and, as the van approached her, she and Ted pelted it with rotten apples. In seconds the windshield was splattered with wormy apple pulp. The minivan started weaving wildly. In the back, Dan started weaving from side to side. He resembled an out-of-control waterskier.

Shelby's best throw was her last. It went right through the passenger's side window, missed the bald-headed man, and conked the driver on the side of the head.

This was good for two reasons. One, the driver had to slow down because he couldn't see. Then he started to blubber.

"Are you crying?!" the bald-headed man asked in disbelief. "You're a hardened criminal! Hardened criminals don't cry!"

The second positive effect Shelby's last apple had was that the driver decided to leave the cemetery. He headed back down Hulbert Street, hung a left on Church (again ignoring the stop sign), and then turned right onto Filkins.

"What are you doing?" demanded the bald-headed man. "This takes us right back to the museum!"

This was true.

"Well, excuse *me*," the driver shouted back. "These are the only streets I know! The side of my head hurts and I'm all gooey!"

"And you're still crying! Stop that!"

The driver snuffled and swiped at the apple pulp on his face with the back of his hand.

Going downhill presented a different set of problems for Dan. Instead of the velvet rope being tight, it was slack. He used gravity to his advantage, though. Acting fast, he flattened himself against the back of the van and, when it went around the corner, he used the momentum to open the back door and climb in. The skateboard went skidding away and was crunched under an oncoming car.

Pete was struggling inside the blanket. Dan quickly uncovered him and began to untie his hands.

"I'll have you out of here in no time, Pete," Dan whispered.

In the front of the van, the two men were still arguing.

"What's that?" the driver asked, alarmed.

"What?"

"That big thing in the middle of the street!"

"It's a cat."

"It's not moving!"

"So?"

"It's staring at me! It's playing chicken with me!"

"It's a *cat!*"

Hearing this, Dan realized they were on Pete's street, and the cat they were talking about was Chester.

"There's a car coming up the hill!" the driver screamed.

"So? If the cat doesn't move, the cat loses the game of chicken!"

"How can you say that?"

"We just kidnapped one kid and maybe did even worse to a bunch of others. You think I care about a stupid cat?"

"But I love animals!"

Chester won the game of chicken. As soon as the other car whizzed by, the driver of the van turned the wheel sharply to the left to avoid hurting the cat. The van spun in a tight circle, teetered for a moment on two wheels, and then ever so gently tipped onto its side. The back doors flew open and Pete and Dan tumbled out, followed by Loretta, the statue of the angel Dan had hidden in the basement.

A police car, siren blaring, was speeding up the hill. Jesse and Dylan had done their job. The driver and the bald-headed man didn't bother to run. Chester thought better of playing another game of chicken with the oncoming squad car. He sauntered off feeling, and rightly so, that he had done more than enough for one day.

THE
SOLUTION

Dan made the newspaper . . .
again. And the national news — as he
had predicted. So did Shelby and Pete.
They were even featured in a weekly
magazine along with Jesse, Dylan, Riley,
Ted, and Brandon. "Young Heroes," the
headline said.

The bald-headed man's real name
was Robert Mansard, and he was an
international art thief. He was believed
to have stolen a Van Gogh from a
museum in Amsterdam and a Picasso
from one in Portugal. He had seen
Dan's picture, the one taken with

Loretta in the newspaper with the headline "Death Stalks Local Boy." He had instantly recognized the statue. The bronze angel was the fabled, long-lost masterpiece of Italian artist Rudolpho Graciano.

Mansard had been looking for the angel for years. The night that he had planned to swoop in and steal her from the garden was the same day Dan had moved her to the basement. If Jesse hadn't knocked her over, Mansard would have succeeded and Loretta would have been gone. Of course Dan couldn't help but think that if you didn't *know* you had something valuable and you lost it, it might not be much of a loss, but that was the kind of shifty thinking that had gotten him into so much trouble in the first place.

As it happened, Miss Alma said the dent in Loretta's arm had been there for years. Dan just hadn't noticed it before.

When Dan reread the threatening notes, he realized that they weren't referring to the skeleton or to David Eckert. They were about the angel. Dan had to admit he had interpreted them incorrectly and jumped to the wrong conclusion. He had seen and heard and understood only what he wanted to see and hear and understand. Part of wisdom, he realized, was sticking to the facts and allowing the facts to speak for themselves.

And Jesus grew in wisdom . . .

"And Dan grew in shortsightedness and self-inflicted ignorance," Dan muttered as he wrote a letter to his father in which he admitted everything he had done, taking full responsibility.

Or did he? Wasn't there something that still had to happen? Wasn't there someone who still needed an apology?

Dan hopped on his skateboard and headed to Eckert House. He entered through the back and climbed the servants' stairs to the third floor. He was still avoiding Mrs. Doheny because every time she saw Dan, she threw her arms around him, cried, and went on and on about how brave he was. "And to think I was going to serve that man our best oolong tea in our best English china!" she would say. "With real cream."

Dan knew that anything brave he had done was only because he had made so many mistakes in the first place.

Miss Alma was in her office. Dan knocked on the open door. She looked up, but didn't say anything.

Dan knew this wasn't going to be easy, but he also knew that it shouldn't be.

"I don't know where to begin. I came to apologize," he said. "The things we thought about you, bringing the police here, lying. I'm sorry."

Miss Alma looked at him for a long time. When she finally spoke, she didn't say what Dan had expected at all.

"Do you have any questions for me, Mr. Pruitt?"

After some thought, he said, "Two."

"The first?" she asked, sensing he needed some help.

"Will you ever forgive me?"

"I will," she answered simply. "And I do."

Dan fought an impulse to cry. She seemed to sense this, too.

"Your second question?"

"Will you tell me about David Eckert?"

"Come with me," she said, rising from her desk. She led Dan down the hall to the door that concealed the staircase to the attic. She unlocked the door, climbed the stairs, stopped at the first landing, and unlocked the door to the little tower room. They both stepped inside.

"I believe you're familiar with this room," she said with a trace of a smile on her face. She looked around, as if remembering it as it had been so many years before.

"There *was* a hidden David Eckert," she began. "I knew him well. And although you got some of it right, there was no murder. Remember, Dan, there's no worse lie than a misunderstood truth." She looked down at her hands, then walked over to a window and looked out. Her face reflected a deep sadness.

Miss Alma's story *was* sad. The David Eckert born in 1925 suffered from Down syndrome. Dan knew what that was. Back in his other school, a boy with Down syndrome, named Austin, was in a Special Needs class. Austin and Dan had eaten lunch together a few times. Dan's mom told him that Austin would always seem to be about six or seven years old, no matter how old or how big he got.

"David was the sweetest boy who ever lived," Miss Alma said. "But his parents were embarrassed, as if being born different was a stain on the family. They kept him locked in this room most of his life. Occasionally they'd let him go out if no one was in the park or if it was raining."

"The boy in the diary met him," Dan said.

"Yes."

"His mother called him a Chinaman. What was that about?"

"Back then, Down syndrome children were called Mongoloids. Mongolia is—"

"Near China," Dan said, understanding the origin of the name. He remembered that Austin's eyes had a slight upturned look to them, as though he might be from Asia.

"A horrible name! A hateful name! Thank goodness we've gotten past that," Miss Alma said.

She explained that David's parents had another son and named him David, too, as if the first one didn't even exist. "Which, in their eyes, he didn't." It was clear from her tone that she found this shameful.

"I came here in 1941, when I was . . . well, let's just say I was young."

"You were sixteen," Dan offered.

Miss Alma didn't seem pleased by his calculation.

"Mr. Pruitt, when a woman chooses not to comment on her age, it's wise to respect that choice."

"Yes, ma'am."

Miss Alma said she was from a poor family, and that she had earned her living as a caregiver. She explained that in 1942, David's parents moved to Florida and left him behind with his grandparents. "David," she explained, "was very much aware of what they had done and cried himself to sleep every night.

"He died less than a year later, in August of 1943. And I believe he mostly died of a broken heart."

The story of Ethel Eckert and Mario Martini was also sad. They had fallen in love and had planned to elope.

"Let me guess," Dan interrupted. "On the night of August 5."

"Yes. A terrible night," Miss Alma said in a whisper. "David had caught a cold a few days earlier, and it quickly developed into pneumonia. He died right around ten that night."

Miss Alma stopped for a moment as she looked to where Dan guessed David's bed had stood.

"Of course Mario and Ethel had no idea. They were totally caught up in their own plans for that night. It was Hollis Eckert, Ethel's grandfather, who discovered Mario in the upstairs of the house, just as Mario and Ethel were about to make their escape. A terrible fight broke out, and a small fire started when a candle was knocked over. Ethel's grandmother panicked and called the fire department and an ambulance, but the fire was extinguished before they arrived.

"That's what we walked into when the nurse and I came down with the news of David's death. Mr. Eckert saw the look on our faces and knew immediately what had happened. He spoke quietly to the ambulance crew, who then followed Nurse Peggy back up to David's room. I was trying to calm Ethel down and get her back to her room, but she was hysterical — and grew even more so when she saw David's body being removed. That's how she learned he had died."

Dan felt sorry for that frightened teenage girl of so many years ago.

"It took me decades to find out what went on between Mario and Mr. Eckert after I got Ethel back to her room. To put it bluntly, Mr. Eckert threatened him."

It all made sense. With Miss Alma laying it out as she did, Dan could picture the whole thing. Hollis Eckert had a poor boy in front of him who was planning to run away with his granddaughter. He had what could be described as a suspicious fire in the upstairs hall, and a body had been whisked away out the back door. Hollis Eckert had offered

Mario a deal. Leave Ethel and Freemont or stay and face charges of arson and murder.

"Hollis Eckert was a powerful man. He was rich enough to make it look like Mario Martini had killed David," Miss Alma said matter-of-factly. "Mario left Freemont the next morning. In his pocket was David Eckert's birth certificate, a document he had planned to use to prove he was eighteen and old enough to marry Ethel. Instead, he changed his name and used it to enlist in the Navy. He was killed in battle just before Christmas.

"As for Ethel, she had a complete nervous break-down. I accompanied her back to Savannah and took care of her for almost a year. Her grandfather tried to cover up what had happened that night by getting his sister-in-law to print false stories in her society column. It backfired. People knew little bits of information and put them together in a story far more sinister than the real one."

Dan looked away, embarrassed.

"You're not the only one who bears some respon-sibility here, Mr. Pruitt."

Dan looked up in surprise.

"I could have set the story straight any number of times," Miss Alma said, "but I didn't. I thought the past was the past, and let the dead rest in peace. But the dead can't rest in peace if the living don't tell the truth."

Dan nodded. He knew now there is no wisdom without truth.

But there was still one question unanswered.

"Miss Alma, whose skeleton did I dig up?"

"I don't know. Let's find out."

An hour later, Dan and Miss Alma sat in the coroner's office as he read them his report. "Female, aged sixty to seventy, I'd say. Died in the mid-1800s."

The coroner explained that the skeleton Dan dug up was one that had been used for medical training purposes.

"How do you know that?" Dan asked.

The coroner pointed out that the autopsy had found microscopic fibers left by the cords, and residue left by the glue used to keep the skeleton together.

"Otherwise, the doctor studying the skeleton would just have a heap of bones."

"So there wasn't a murder!" Dan exclaimed.

"No. Why it was buried there is anyone's guess, but we can certainly rule out foul play."

"Foul play, yes. Foolishness, no," Miss Alma said.

Dan thought Miss Alma was poking fun at him,

but when they got back to Eckert House, he understood what she meant. Miss Alma took Dan into the library and stood him in front of the picture in which everyone was dressed as Sherlock Holmes.

"Tell me what you see," she said.

A few minutes later, Dan had it. The "whopping body of evidence" promised in the invitation was the skeleton! It had to be! It was buried out back as part of the elaborate party, but never discovered. The skeleton must have belonged to the first David Eckert—Dr. David Eckert.

"That one," said Miss Alma, pointing to the most noticeable woman in the photo, "was Lydia Eckert Tucker. The silliest woman who ever lived in this house. She was personally responsible for spending over half of her grandfather's fortune. Disgraceful."

"Well," sighed Dan, "I guess that's it."

But it wasn't. A week later, Dan, Shelby, Pete, and Miss Alma were in the cemetery above the town standing next to a large memorial topped by a marble angel. It was here that most of the Eckerts were buried. It was here, Miss Alma explained, that David Eckert was secretly buried in 1943. His parents were too ashamed to put his name on the tombstone, an omission Miss Alma had decided to correct.

The workman finished chiseling the last number into the stone. "David James Eckert, 1925–1943." He nodded to Miss Alma, picked up his tools, and left.

"Mr. Pruitt, would you like to say a prayer?" Miss Alma asked.

Dan took off his cap.

"Lord, David Eckert is already in your arms. So are a lot of other people who knew him. I get really sad when I think about him looking out his window, watching life go by, wanting to be a part of it. It sounds like he was a really nice guy, and we trust he's having a better time with you than he did down here with us. That's good. There's so much we need to be smarter about. And I'm not just talking about people like David. I'm talking about a lot of things. Please help us to do that. Help us to be smart enough to see the things you want us to see and give us the courage to do the things you need us to do. Amen."

They all added their "amens," then turned and walked back down the hill. Miss Alma said good-bye to them in front of Pete's house. However, before she continued on to the museum, she had one more thing to say to Dan.

"Mr. Pruitt, by my calculations, you still owe me forty-seven hours and twenty-three minutes of work. I'll see you tomorrow afternoon."

"Yes, ma'am,"

This time Dan smiled.

One mystery had been solved, but there was still the question of who wrote the diary. And who knew how many other mysteries might still be hidden within the walls of Eckert House.

What is  SOUL GEAR?

Based on Luke 2:52:
"And Jesus grew in wisdom and stature, and in favor with God and men (NIV)."

2:52 is designed just for boys 8-12! This verse is one of the only verses in the Bible that provides a glimpse of Jesus as a young boy. Who doesn't wonder what Jesus was like as a kid?

Become smarter, stronger, deeper, and cooler as you develop into a young man of God with 2:52 Soul Gear™!

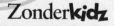

The 2:52 Soul Gear™ takes a closer look by focusing on the four major areas of development highlighted in Luke 2:52:

"Wisdom" = mental/emotional = **Smarter**

"Stature" = physical = **Stronger**

"Favor with God" = spiritual = **Deeper**

"Favor with men" = social = **Cooler**

2:52 Mysteries of Eckert House

Three friends seek to uncover the hidden mysteries of Eckert House in this four-book series filled with adventure, mystery, and intrigue.

2:52 Mysteries of Eckert House:
A Stranger, a Thief & a Pack of Lies [Book 2]

Written by Chris Auer
Many secrets lie within the walls of Eckert House,
but no one is prepared when a stranger, claiming
to be the sole heir of Eckert House, shows up.
Softcover 0-310-70871-0

2:52 Mysteries of Eckert House:
The Chinese Puzzle Box [Book 3]

Written by Chris Auer
Dan and his friends discover a riddle hidden in an ancient
Chinese puzzle box, but someone is trying to get them out
of Eckert House. Whoever it is will stop at nothing to get
rid of them!
Softcover 0-310-70872-9

2:52 Mysteries of Eckert House:
The Forgotten Room [Book 4]

Written by Chris Auer
Dan Pruitt's certain he's found a hidden room. But when he
and his friends set out to find it, they uncover more than a room.
What they find will ultimately lead to danger; how will they
keep their secret safe and protect themselves too?
Softcover 0-310-70873-7

Available now at your local bookstore!

Zonderkidz.

The 2:52 Boys Bible–
the "ultimate manual" for boys

The 2:52 Boys Bible, NIV
Features written by Rick Osborne

Become more like Jesus mentally, physically, spiritually, and social–Smarter, Stronger, Deeper, and Cooler—with the *2:52 Boys Bible!*

Hardcover 0-310-70320-4
Softcover 0-310-70552-5

Also from Inspirio . . .

CD Holder   ISBN: 0-310-99033-5

Book & Bible Holder

Med   ISBN: 0-310-98823-3

Large ISBN: 0-310-98824-1

inspirio
The gift group of Zondervan

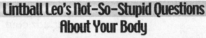

We want to hear from you. Please send your comments about this book to us in care of zreview@zondervan.com. Thank you.

Zonder**kidz**.

Grand Rapids, MI 49530
www.zonderkidz.com